PUFFIN BOOKS

HERE COME THE TWINS

Janet and Jimmy are twins, and they like it – getting up to mischief is more fun in pairs! Not that they necessarily always want to do the same things. Jimmy, for example, likes things that are real, whereas Janet often prefers to pretend. When Jimmy digs a big hole all by himself using a real shovel, Janet pretends it's a nest, until their father comes up with another idea which fills up the hole for good.

There's no knowing what game they will think up next, but one thing is certain: with Janet and Jimmy around, life is never dull!

Beverly Cleary was born in Oregon, USA. She found herself in the low reading circle at school, an experience that has given her sympathy for the problems of struggling readers. It was her school librarian who suggested that she should write for children when she grew up. The idea appealed to her, and she decided she would write funny stories about her neighbourhood and the sort of children she knew. Mrs Cleary followed a career in children's librarianship after graduating from the University of Washington. Married with grown-up twins, she now lives in California, writing and pursuing her hobbies of travel and needlework.

HERE COME THE TWINS

BEVERLY CLEARY

Illustrated by Thelma Lambert

PUFFIN BOOKS

PUFFIN BOOKS

Published by the Penguin Group
Penguin Books Ltd, 27 Wrights Lane, London W8 5TZ, England
Penguin Books USA Inc., 375 Hudson Street, New York, New York 10014, USA
Penguin Books Australia Ltd, Ringwood, Victoria, Australia
Penguin Books Canada Ltd, 10 Alcorn Avenue, Toronto, Ontario, Canada M4V 3B2
Penguin Books (NZ) Ltd, 182–190 Wairau Road, Auckland 10, New Zealand

Penguin Books Ltd, Registered Offices: Harmondsworth, Middlesex, England

The Real Hole and *Two Dog Biscuits* first published in Great Britain
as *Here Come the Twins* by Hamish Hamilton Children's Books 1989
Remaining text first published in Great Britain as
The Twins Again by Hamish Hamilton Children's Books 1989
Published in one volume in Puffin Books 1990
10 9 8 7 6 5 4

Printed in England by Clays Ltd, St Ives plc
Filmset in Baskerville

Chapter One

Jimmy and Janet are twins. This
means they have the same mother,
the same father, and the same
birthday, too. Jimmy always has
Janet to play with, and Janet always
has Jimmy to play with. Even
though Jimmy and Janet are both
four years old, they do not always
like the same things.

Janet likes pretend things. She

likes to pretend that a block is a cup of tea or that two paper bags are a pair of boots.

But Jimmy — Jimmy likes real things. He doesn't want to play with a toy hammer and toy nails. He wants to play with a real grown-up hammer and real grown-up nails. When Jimmy's father brings him a present, the first thing Jimmy asks is, "Is it real?"

One morning Jimmy said to his father, "I want to dig a hole. I want to dig the biggest hole in the world."

"That's a good idea," said Jimmy's father, and he found a place in the corner of the garden where Jimmy could dig a hole.

Jimmy took his toy shovel and

began to dig. He put the shovel into
the earth and pushed it down with
his foot, the way he had seen his
father dig. When he tried to lift the
dirt — *snap, crack* — the handle of
his shovel broke.

"Daddy! My shovel broke," cried
Jimmy. "I need a real shovel."

"The real shovel is too big," said
Jimmy's father, "but you can try."
He brought Jimmy the real shovel,
which was much bigger than Jimmy.
Jimmy worked and worked, but the
real shovel was too big and heavy
for him. The hole Jimmy was
digging was hardly a hole at all.

4

"I have an idea," said Jimmy's father. He went into the garage and came out with a shovel that was just Jimmy's size. "I had forgotten we had this," he said.

"Is it real?" asked Jimmy.

"Yes, it's real," answered Jimmy's father. "This is the kind of shovel soldiers use to dig trenches. It is called a trench digger."

"Real soldiers?" asked Jimmy.

"Real soldiers," answered his father.

While Janet played on her swing, Jimmy began to dig. The real shovel that real soldiers used was just the

right size for Jimmy. He could never
break the handle of this shovel.

He pushed the shovel into the
ground, lifted out the earth, and
tossed it out of the hole. Push, lift,
toss. This was the way Jimmy
wanted to dig.

When the milkman brought the
milk, he said to Jimmy, "Say, that's
a real shovel you have there! And

that's a great big hole you're digging!"

"I'm digging the biggest hole in the world," answered Jimmy, and he went on digging.

"What a big hole!" said Jimmy's mother, when she came outside to tell Jimmy and Janet that lunch was ready. Then she brushed the earth off Jimmy's jeans and emptied the

earth out of Jimmy's shoes.

After lunch, while Janet galloped
around on her hobbyhorse, Jimmy
went right on digging. Push, lift,
toss. The hole was almost up to his
knees when his mother came outside,
brushed the earth off his jeans,
emptied the dirt out of his shoes, and
took him inside for his nap.

Chapter Two

Jimmy was so tired from digging all morning that he had a good long nap. When he woke up he climbed out of his bed in a hurry, so he could go outside and dig in his hole again.

But when Jimmy opened the back door, he discovered that Janet was already awake. She was not only awake, she was out in the garden sitting in his hole!

"That's my hole!" said Jimmy.

"I am a little bird sitting on a nest," said Janet.

"That is not a nest!" yelled Jimmy. "That is my hole, and I want to dig in it!"

"Children!" said the twins' mother. "Janet, let Jimmy have his hole. It's his, because he dug it."

"I just wanted to borrow Jimmy's hole for a little while," said Janet, as she climbed out and went to play on the slide.

"I don't want Janet to borrow my hole," said Jimmy, and he began to dig with his real shovel. He dug and dug. Push, lift, toss. The hole grew deeper and deeper. Pretty soon it was up to Jimmy's knees. Still

Jimmy dug. He had never worked so hard, but of course he had never had a real shovel to work with before. Then some earth around the edge of the hole fell into the hole and buried Jimmy's shoes. Jimmy was not discouraged.

He pulled his feet out of the earth, shovelled the earth out of the hole, and went on digging.

"Jimmy, you look so hot and tired," said his mother. "Why don't you have a rest?"

"No," said Jimmy. "I'm digging the biggest hole in the world."

Soon Jimmy's mother and father came to look at the hole.

"My goodness," said his mother. "What are you going to do with

such a great big hole?"

"We could pretend it is a place to catch fish," said Janet. "I could tie a string to a stick and pretend I am catching fish."

"No," said Jimmy. "It isn't a place to catch fish. It is a real big hole."

"What are you going to do with your real hole?" asked his father.

"We could pretend it is a place where baby rabbits live," said Janet. "I could get in the hole and pretend I am a baby rabbit."

"No!" said Jimmy. "It isn't a place where baby rabbits live. It is a real hole, and I made it with a real shovel."

Then the lady who lived next door came over to see Jimmy's hole. "What a big hole!" she said. "What are you going to do with such a great big hole?"

Jimmy did not know what he was going to do with such a great big hole. Muffy, the dog who lived next door, came over and sniffed the hole.

"Muffy could bury bones in the hole," said Janet.

"No!" said Jimmy. "Muffy can dig his own hole."

Then the man who lived next door came to see Jimmy's hole.

"Say, that is a big hole!" he said.

"What are you going to do with such a big hole?"

Everybody thought Jimmy should do something with his hole. Everybody but Jimmy. He liked his hole just the way it was.

"I am going to keep my hole," he said.

"I'm afraid not," said his father. "If you or Janet ran across the garden and fell into the hole, you might get hurt."

Jimmy looked at his father. Not keep his real hole that he had dug with his real shovel?

"I want to keep my hole," he said.

"Now Jimmy," said his father. "I don't want you or Janet to get hurt."

"You said I could dig a big hole,"

Jimmy reminded him.

"Yes, but I didn't know you could dig such a big hole," answered his father. This made Jimmy feel better. His father hadn't known he could dig such a big hole.

"There must be something we could do with such a nice hole," said Jimmy's mother. "It's a pity not to use it for something, when Jimmy has worked so hard." So Jimmy and Janet and their mother and father thought and thought.

What could they do with such a big hole?

"I know!" said Jimmy's father.

"What?" asked Jimmy and Janet.

"You wait and see. It's a surprise," answered their father, and he backed the car out of the garage and drove away.

"What do you suppose he's going to get?" asked the twins' mother.

"Is it a big water pipe?" asked Jimmy.

"Is it a family of baby rabbits?" asked Janet.

"I don't know," answered their mother. "We will have to wait and see."

After a while Jimmy and Janet's father came back. When he got out of the car he took something out of the back seat. It was a tree growing in a big pot.

"Is it a real tree?" asked Jimmy.

"Yes, it's a real spruce tree,"

answered his father, "and your hole is just the right size to plant it in."

Jimmy grabbed his shovel. He wanted to help plant a real tree in his real hole.

His father took the tree out of the pot and set it in the hole.

With the hose they watered the roots of the tree.

Then they filled the hole with earth.

"Now we have a real tree growing

in our garden," said Jimmy's mother.

"We can pretend it's a Christmas tree," said Janet.

"It is a Christmas tree," said her father. "This year we can have two Christmas trees, one in the house and one in the garden."

"You didn't know I could dig a hole for a tree," said Jimmy, who was pleased with what he had done.

"No, we didn't," said Jimmy's mother. Then she brushed the earth off Jimmy's jeans and emptied the earth out of Jimmy's shoes.

"It was a real grown-up hole," Jimmy said proudly.

"He's right," said Jimmy's father. "It certainly was. A real grown-up hole!"

Chapter Three

Now that Jimmy and Janet are four
years old they can do lots of things.
They can draw pictures of funny
bugs and birthday cakes and eggs in
a nest.

They can sing *Skip to My Lou.*
They can swing themselves up high,
and they can swat flies.

Janet always has Jimmy to play
with her on the swing and Jimmy

always has Janet to sit on the other end of the see-saw.

"I think twins are a very nice arrangement," said Mummy.

"What does 'very nice arrangement' mean?" asked Janet, who liked big words.

"It means I am glad I have twins," answered Mummy. Jimmy and Janet think twins are a nice arrangement, too.

One morning Jimmy and Janet went to see Mrs Robbins, the lady next door, and her dog Muffy. When they came home Jimmy was carrying a dog biscuit shaped like a bone. Janet was carrying a dog biscuit shaped like a bone, too.

"See what Mrs Robbins gave us,"

they said.

"What are you going to do with two dog biscuits?" asked Mummy.

"I'm going to keep my dog biscuit," said Jimmy.

"I'm going to keep my dog

biscuit, too," said Janet. "It is a
nice little dog biscuit."

"All right," said Mummy, "but
be sure you don't eat the dog
biscuits. Dog biscuits are for dogs."

Janet laid her dog biscuit on a
chair. Jimmy laid his dog biscuit on
the sofa. When Mummy started to
sit on the sofa, she asked, "Whose
dog biscuit is this?"

"My dog biscuit," answered
Jimmy, and put his dog biscuit on
the kitchen table. Janet put her dog
biscuit on the kitchen table, too. She
did not want Mummy to sit on her
dog biscuit.

At lunchtime Mummy said, "Put
your dog biscuits away, children. I
don't want you to get mixed up and
eat them for lunch. Dog biscuits are
for dogs."

Jimmy and Janet put their dog
biscuits in their pockets.

27

After lunch and naps Mummy said,
"It's time for some clean clothes."
When Jimmy took off his jeans, his
dog biscuit fell out of his pocket.
When Janet took off her dress, her
dog biscuit fell out of her pocket, too.

"My goodness," said Mummy.
"Every place I look I see dog biscuits.
Why don't you take the dog biscuits
next door and give them to Muffy?"

"Muffy has dog biscuits," said
Janet. "He has a big bag of them."

"Then give the dog biscuits to
some other dog," said Mummy.

"Dogs don't come to our house,"
said Jimmy.

"Then let's go and find a dog," said Mummy. "Put on your clean clothes, and we'll go for a walk and find a dog that would like two dog biscuits."

Chapter Four

So Jimmy and Janet, wearing their
clean clothes, went for a walk with
Mummy. "Be on the lookout for a
dog," said Mummy.

"What does 'be on the lookout'
mean?" asked Janet.

"It means to watch for
something," answered Mummy.
Jimmy and Janet and Mummy were
on the lookout for a dog.

The first dog they met was a big brown dog.

"I don't want to give my dog biscuit to a brown dog," said Jimmy.

"I don't want to give my dog biscuit to a big dog," said Janet.

"Oh dear," said Mummy. "I suppose we will have to find another dog."

After a while they met a small white dog.

"I'm sure this dog is very hungry," said Mummy.

The little dog barked. *Yip-yip-yip*.

"No," said Janet. "That is not a nice dog. I want to give my nice little dog biscuit to a nice little dog."

"Oh dear," said Mummy. "I

suppose we will have to find another dog."

After a while they met a big black dog.

"I'm sure this dog would like two dog biscuits," said Mummy.

The dog was hungry. He barked. *Woof-woof-woof.*

"No," said Jimmy. "I don't like
dogs that bark."

"Oh dear," said Mummy. "I
suppose we will have to find another
dog."

They went on walking. They met big dogs, little dogs, smooth dogs, curly dogs, dogs that sniffed, and dogs that wagged their tails. Each time they met a dog Jimmy and Janet said, "No, I don't want to give my dog biscuit to this dog."

"Oh dear," said Mummy. "What are we going to do? It's almost time for Daddy to come home, and we have not found the right dog to give the dog biscuits to. What are we going to do?"

Jimmy and Janet thought and thought. What were they going to do? They did not really want to give their dog biscuits to a dog. If Muffy had his own dog biscuits, other dogs must have dog biscuits, too.

"We could give the dog biscuits to a cat," said Janet and laughed. What a funny idea, dog biscuits for a cat!

"Oh no," said Mummy. "A cat

couldn't eat a dog biscuit, because it would be too hard for his teeth. Dog biscuits are for dogs."

Just the same, on the way home Jimmy and Janet were on the lookout for a cat.

When they were almost home Janet spied a big tabby cat snoozing on a drive in the sunshine.

"There is a cat," she said. "I'm going to give him my dog biscuit."

"I'm afraid that cat does not want your dog biscuit," said Mummy.

Janet tiptoed over to the cat and laid her dog biscuit under his nose. "Here is a present for you, kitty," she said.

The cat opened one eye. He

opened the other eye. He stood up
and stretched. He sniffed the dog
biscuit.

Then he sat down and began to
eat. It was hard work for him to eat
such a hard biscuit, but he crunched
and munched and soon the biscuit
was gone.

The cat licked his whiskers,
looked around, and said, "Meow."

"He liked my dog biscuit," said
Janet. "He's saying thank you."

"He wants another dog biscuit," said Jimmy.

"Here, kitty. Here is another present for you." The cat crunched and munched Jimmy's dog biscuit, and when it was all gone he sat up and began to wash.

"You didn't know a cat would eat dog biscuits," Jimmy said to Mummy. "You said dog biscuits were for dogs." He and Janet laughed. What fun it was to know something a grown-up didn't know!

"No, I didn't know a cat would eat dog biscuits, but now I know it," said Mummy, and she laughed, too. "Oh look, there's Daddy coming home from work."

"Daddy! Daddy!" shouted Janet, running along the pavement to meet him. "We gave our dog biscuits to a cat and he ate them!"

"Daddy, Daddy!" shouted Jimmy, running along the pavement to meet him. "Mummy said the cat wouldn't eat the dog biscuits, but he did! She didn't know!"

Daddy caught Jimmy and Janet and picked them both up at the same time. "Your mother didn't know a cat would eat dog biscuits!" he exclaimed. "What a funny joke!"

Chapter Five

"I can't find the thingamajigs,"
Mummy said, when Jimmy fell
down and grazed his knee. "What
happened to the thingamajigs?"

Thingamajigs was a word Mummy
sometimes used when she was
excited or in a hurry. Janet, who
was Jimmy's twin sister, enjoyed
finding out what thingamajigs meant

each time her mother used the word.
This time it meant plaster.

While Mummy took care of
Jimmy's knee, Janet found a red
plastic paper clip, a little wheel, and
a shiny bead. They were just right
to hold in her hand. "Are these
thingamajigs?" she asked.

Mummy laughed and said, "Yes,
you could call those thingamajigs."

Janet carried her things around all morning. She showed them to Mr Lemon, the postman. "See my thingamajigs," she said.

"Well, what do you know? Thingamajigs!" Mr Lemon sounded surprised.

At lunchtime, Janet laid her plastic paper clip, her little wheel, and her shiny bead on a chair in the living room and said, "I don't want Jimmy to touch these things."

"They're just old stuff," said Jimmy, who wanted very much to touch them, so he did. He touched them every time Janet wasn't looking. He liked to hold them, too.

He touched them until Janet caught him at it and said, "Jimmy,

43

those are *my* thingamajigs."

"No," said Jimmy, holding on to them.

"Mummy, Jimmy won't give me my thingamajigs," said Janet, "and I asked him in a nice, polite voice."

"I'm not hurting them," said Jimmy, who could be stubborn.

"Jimmy, give me my thingamajigs!" yelled Janet. Her voice was not polite at all.

"No," said Jimmy, and he turned
his back.

Janet pushed Jimmy.

Jimmy yelled, "Janet is pushing
me!" Then he pushed Janet.

"Children!" cried Mummy as she
came out of the kitchen. "Stop this
at once. Jimmy, give Janet her little
things. You can find toys of your
own."

Jimmy threw Janet's things on the floor. "I don't want other toys!" he shouted.

Janet picked up her things and put them back on the chair. "I don't want Jimmy to touch my thingamajigs," she said.

Mummy said, "Janet, you cannot leave them on that chair. When Daddy comes home, he wants to sit on the chair. He doesn't want to sit on your toys. If you don't want

Jimmy to touch your things, you should put them away."

So Janet found a paper bag in the kitchen. She put the red plastic paper clip, the little wheel, and the shiny bead into the bag, wrapped a rubber band around the top, and put it in her cot. "Now Jimmy can't touch my thingamajigs," she said.

"I don't want to touch Janet's things," said Jimmy, but he *did* want to touch them, more than anything.

Chapter Six

The next day, Janet found a cotton-reel, a doll's shoe, and a smooth green stone. She carried her new little things around while Jimmy pretended to put air in the tyres of his lorry. She showed them to Mr Lemon when he brought the mail. Then she laid her little things on a chair and went into Mummy and Daddy's room to help Mummy make the big bed. When she came back, Jimmy was not playing with his lorry. He was holding her cotton-reel, her doll's shoe and her smooth green stone.

"Jimmy is touching my thingamajigs!" Janet cried. "He took them from the blue chair!"

"Children, I am at my wit's end," said Mummy.

"What does 'at my wit's end' mean?" asked Janet.

"It means I don't know what to do," answered Mummy. "Jimmy, give Janet her things."

Jimmy threw the toys on the floor. "I am too big for those things," he said. "They're just junk."

"They're not junk," said Janet. "They are my treasures."

Jimmy only pretended to play with his lorry while she picked up her treasures and laid them on the blue chair again.

"Janet," said Mummy, "you cannot leave your things on the blue chair. I do not want to sit on your toys. I told you if you don't want Jimmy to touch them, you should put them away."

"I am at my wit's end," said Janet.
Then she found another paper
bag in the kitchen. She put her
cotton-reel, her doll's shoe, and her
smooth green stone into her paper
bag. She put a rubber band around
the top of the bag and put it in her
cot.

"Now Jimmy can't touch my
thingamajigs," she said.

The next day the same thing happened with a feather, a piece of pink wool and an old lipstick case. And the day after that the same thing happened with a little stick, a pretty leaf, and an empty snail shell. Every day Janet found little things, and every day she put them into paper bags in her cot, where Jimmy could not touch them.

One day Mummy said, "Janet, your cot is full of paper bags. When you go to bed, you rustle like a mouse in a wastepaper basket. Don't you want to share some of your

paper bags with Jimmy?"

"No," said Janet as she climbed
over the side of her cot. "These are
my paper bags."

"Oh dear, what are we going to
do?" asked Mummy. "Janet's cot is
so full of paper bags she rustles like
a mouse in a wastepaper basket.
There is scarcely room for her to
sleep. What are we going to do?"

"Paper bags are silly," said
Jimmy as he climbed over the rail of
his cot. Neither twin would let

Mummy lower the side of a cot.
Climbing over the side was fun.

"Paper bags are not silly," said
Janet. "Paper bags are nice."

"But Janet, you have too many,"
said Mummy. "We will have to find
another place for all your paper
bags."

"I like being a mouse in a

wastepaper basket," said Janet, and
she went right on finding little
things and putting them in paper
bags in her cot. Every night she said,
"*Squeak-squeak*. I am a little mouse."

"*Grr-grr*. I am a fierce bear," said
Jimmy. He did not sound like a
fierce bear. He sounded like a cross
boy.

Chapter Seven

Then one morning Mummy said,
"Today we are going to have a
surprise."

"Is it strawberries?" asked Jimmy.

"Is it a nice soft kitten?" asked
Janet.

"No, it isn't strawberries or a nice
soft kitten," answered Mummy.
"You wait and see."

56

Jimmy and Janet thought and thought, but they could not think what Mummy's surprise could be.

"If you watch out the front window, you will see it sometime this morning," said Mummy.

Jimmy and Janet watched out the front window. "When is it going to come? When is it going to come?" they asked over and over again. They saw a boy riding a bicycle, a girl skipping, and a lady carrying a shopping bag. They saw cars, a breakdown lorry, and a school bus, but they did not see a surprise. After a while they grew tired of watching and turned their little table upside down and pretended it was a boat.

And then, when the twins

happened to look out the window, a big delivery lorry came slowly down the street, paused, and turned into the drive – Jimmy and Janet's drive. Two men got out of the lorry. They opened the back, lifted something out, and set it on the grass. It was a bed.

They lifted out another bed and set it on the grass, too. Grown-up beds!

"Beds!" shouted Jimmy and Janet. "Mummy, are these beds for us?"

"Yes," answered Mummy. "You are growing up. It is time for you to have big beds."

The men carried one bed into the house and set it on Janet's side of the bedroom. They carried the other bed into the house and set it on

Jimmy's side of the room. "There you
are, kids," one of them said. "Sleep
tight, and don't let the bedbugs bite."

Jimmy and Janet bounced up and down on their new grown-up beds while Mummy stood in the hall and watched. Then Jimmy stopped bouncing.

"What is Janet going to do with

her paper bags?" he asked. "They
will fall off her bed."

Janet stopped bouncing. She took
her paper bags from her cot and
piled them on her new bed. When
she climbed back on her bed, paper
bags slid off all over the floor.

"Ha-ha," said Jimmy.

"Jimmy can have my old paper
bags," said Janet. "I am not a
mouse. I am a big girl, and I sleep
in a big bed."

"I don't want Janet's paper
bags," said Jimmy. "I am too big to
play with bits of junk."

"So am I," said Janet.

The twins began to bounce again.
"We are big! We are big!" they
sang, while Mummy tried to gather

up all of Janet's paper bags. Then Jimmy and Janet heard Mr Lemon poking letters through the letterbox in the front door. They jumped off their beds and ran to meet him.

"Mr Lemon! Mr Lemon!" they shouted when they opened the door. "We have big beds! We have big beds!"

"Wow! Big beds!" said Mr Lemon.

Jimmy and Janet could tell he was really surprised.

"You *are* growing up!" said Mr Lemon. "I never would have guessed."

Growing up — that was what Jimmy and Janet wanted more than anything in the whole world. "We are growing up!" they shouted. "We are growing up!"

Chapter Eight

"When are my feet going to grow up?" Jimmy asked one morning as he wiggled his toes.

"They're growing all the time," said Mummy. "They have grown so much that it is time to go to the shoe shop and talk to Mr Markle about new shoes."

"For me, too?" asked Janet.

"For both of you," said Mummy.

"Our feet are growing up!" shouted Jimmy. "Our feet are growing up!"

"New shoes, new shoes, we're going to get new shoes!" said Janet. Then she said, "And I'm going to surprise Mr Lemon with new shoes when he brings the post." Janet liked to surprise people, especially Mr Lemon.

Mummy and the twins drove to the shoe shop, where they sat on

three chairs in a row, with Mummy
in the middle.

Mr Markle pulled up a stool and
sat down in front of them. "What
will my favourite customers have
today?" he asked.

"Shoes," said Jimmy. "Our feet
are growing up."

"You don't say," said Mr Markle.
He felt the toes of Jimmy's and
Janet's shoes. Then he took off their
shoes and asked each of them to

stand on his measuring stick while he slid the wooden piece to the tips of their toes.

Mr Markle shook his head. "Sorry," he said. "You kids aren't ready for new shoes."

No new shoes! Jimmy and Janet looked at Mummy and said, "You told us we were ready for new shoes."

Mummy sighed. "Mothers can be wrong sometimes," she said. That made Jimmy and Janet feel better — a little, but not much.

Mr Markle looked disappointed, too. He sniffed and rubbed his eyes with his fists and looked so silly that Jimmy and Janet almost smiled.

Janet leaned against Mummy. "I won't have a surprise for Mr Lemon today," she said and looked very, very sad. "Mr Lemon likes me to surprise him."

"We'll think of another surprise," said Mummy.

"But it won't be new shoes," answered Janet.

"I *want* new shoes," said Jimmy.

"Now, Jimmy," said Mummy. "You're a big boy."

"No, I'm not!" said Jimmy. "My

feet didn't grow up."

"How would you each like a balloon?" asked Mr Markle.

Jimmy and Janet took the balloons, but they did not really want balloons. They wanted new shoes.

"You know something?" said Mr Markle. "We have some boots on special offer."

"We can't buy boots to fit over old shoes," said Mummy.

"But these boots stretch," said Mr Markle. "They will fit over old shoes and new shoes, too. And you know

something else? These boots are red."

Red boots. Jimmy and Janet
looked up at Mummy.

"Good," said Mummy. "Let's
buy new boots."

"For me?" asked Jimmy.

"For me?" asked Janet.

"For both of you," said Mummy.

Mr Markle brought out bright red
boots, which fitted over the old shoes.
"There you are, kids," he said. "Just
what the Easter Bunny ordered."

Jimmy and Janet thought Mr

Markle was such a silly man. They knew Easter was a long time ago.

Jimmy wore his boots, but Janet carried hers in their box. The twins were so happy they didn't even stop to pat the hobbyhorse on their way out the door. Mummy remembered to say "thank you" to Mr Markle.

When Mummy and the twins returned home, they found Mr Lemon

had already delivered the post. Janet hid her box of boots in the cupboard.

"I'm going to save my boots to show Daddy," she said, "and tomorrow I will surprise Mr Lemon."

"Jimmy, don't you want to take off your boots?" asked Mummy.

"No," said Jimmy and ran out into the garden. In a little while he came back. "I can't find any

puddles," he said.

"Of course there aren't any puddles," said Mummy. "It isn't raining."

"When is it going to rain?" asked Jimmy.

"I don't know," answered Mummy. "There aren't any clouds, so it won't rain today."

"Will it rain tomorrow?" asked Jimmy.

"I don't know," said Mummy. "I don't think so."

"The next day?" asked Jimmy.

"I don't know."

Mummy sounded tired as she made sandwiches for lunch.

New boots and no puddles. Jimmy pretended he was walking in

puddles, but he wanted *real* puddles with *real* water. Janet waited and waited for Daddy to come home so she could show him her red boots in their box.

When Daddy came home he was surprised once to see Jimmy wearing new boots, and surprised twice when Janet opened her box to show him her boots. After the surprise, Janet put her boots on, too.

"Our feet didn't grow up," said Jimmy, "and Mummy said they did."

"Don't worry. They will," said Daddy.

Jimmy and Janet wore their boots while they ate their dinner. Their feet were hot, but they didn't care. At bedtime they pulled their boots on over the feet of their sleepsuits.

When Mummy said they could not sleep with boots over their sleepsuits because their feet would be too hot, they slept with their boots on their hands.

Chapter Nine

In the morning Jimmy and Janet
pulled their new boots on over their
old shoes. "My goodness," said
Mummy. "You will wear your boots
out before we have any rain."

This morning Daddy put on an
old pair of trousers and a sweatshirt.

"Are you going to stay home
today?" asked Jimmy as he watched

Daddy shave. He liked to watch so he would know how when he was old enough to shave off whiskers of his own.

"Yes. Today is Saturday," answered Daddy.

Janet, who knew she would never have whiskers like Daddy, was in the kitchen with Mummy. "I wish Mr Lemon would hurry up and come," she said.

After breakfast Jimmy said to Daddy, "If we went for a walk, maybe we could find some puddles."

Daddy smiled. "I'm afraid not, but I know what we can do. Come outside with me."

"I'm going to sit on the front step and watch for Mr Lemon," said Janet.

Daddy backed the car out of the garage. Then he turned on the hose and started to wash the car. Water ran down the drive.

"Puddles!" shouted Jimmy and began to splash. Janet decided Mr Lemon would be surprised to see wet boots when the sun was shining, so she splashed, too.

Mummy stood in the doorway, watching her twins have fun. Daddy turned the hose on the grass and made a big puddle. Jimmy and Janet squished and splashed in the wet grass. Their boots were wet, but their shoes were dry.

Then they saw Mr Lemon coming down the street with his bag full of letters.

"You stay here," Janet told Jimmy.

"I want to surprise Mr Lemon."

"Okay," said Jimmy and went on stomping and splashing.

"Well!" said Mr Lemon when Janet ran to meet him. "Look at those red boots and all those wet footprints when the sun is shining."

Janet was happy because she could see Mr Lemon was really surprised.

When the postman reached the pavement, Jimmy stopped splashing to explain, "My feet didn't grow up. They are still the same size inside my boots."

"Don't worry," said Mr Lemon. "Before you know it, your feet will be bigger than mine."

"They will?" Jimmy looked at Mr Lemon's feet. They were even bigger than Daddy's feet.

"And do you know something?" asked Mr Lemon as he handed Jimmy the letters to carry. "When you get new shoes, those boots will grow to fit."

Now it was Janet's turn to be surprised. "How did you know?" she asked Mr Lemon.

"I've learnt a thing or two in my lifetime," said Mr Lemon.

Jimmy and Janet splashed in their puddle. "We have growing-up feet!" they shouted. "We have growing-up boots, too!"

Mr Lemon said so, and he knew a thing or two.

GEORGE SPEAKS

Dick King-Smith

**Laura's baby brother George was four
weeks old when it happened.**

George looks like an ordinary baby, with
his round red face and squashy nose. But
Laura soon discovers that he's absolutely
extraordinary, and everyone's life is
turned upside down from the day George
speaks!

Hank Prank
and
Hot Henrietta

Jules Older

**You'll never meet a pair *quite* like
Hank Prank and Hot Henrietta!**

What can you do with an impossible duo
like Hank Prank and Hot Henrietta?
Well, their parents and teachers do try
their best to keep them under control –
but not always with much success!

Mrs Pepperpot
in the Magic Wood

Alf Prøysen

**Nine delightfully funny stories about
that incredible shrinking woman,
Mrs Pepperpot!**

How would *you* feel if you suddenly
shrank to the size of a pepperpot? Well,
that's exactly what happens to Mrs
Pepperpot – and always at the most
awkward moments. But it *does* lead her
into a lot of very exciting adventures in
which she meets some very unusual
characters!

Jimmy Tag-Along

Brian Patten

"We'll call you Jimmy Tag-Along, because you'll be wanting to tag along with us on some of our adventures – won't he, Mrs Battyhats?"

Uncle Elliot and Mrs Battyhats are Jimmy's crazy new neighbours. Not only do they look daft and say the oddest things, but they have *real* secret adventures on which Jimmy is always invited...

Also in Young Puffin

Fat Puss and Friends

Harriet Castor

Fat Puss was fat. He had little thin arms, small flat feet, a very short tail and an amazingly fat tummy.

He can't do all sorts of things that his friends can do, but instead of being miserable he finds some special (and funny) things he *can* do – like making friends with mice!

Also in Young Puffin

Brinsly's Dream

Petronella Breinburg

"Football, football, that's all you can think of," said Brinsly's sister.

And she was right. Brinsly just lived for football. He knew his team would have to practise really hard if they were going to win a few matches – and maybe even win the festival trophy!

HELP!

Margaret Gordon

"Help! Help! Help!"

Fred and Flo are very helpful little pigs.
The problem is, the more helpful they try
to be, the more trouble they cause.
Whether they are washing Grandad's car,
looking after Baby or doing the
decorating, disaster is never far away.

THE PIRATE UNCLE

Margaret Mahy

"I *was* a pirate. Now I'm trying to give it up, and I need help."

One summer holiday Caroline and Nicholas meet Uncle Ludovic, who claims to be a pirate trying to mend his ways. Sometimes he certainly does some very piratical things. But soon Caroline hits on a sure way to reform their pirate uncle.

DUSTBIN CHARLIE

Ann Pilling

"Is a skip bigger than a dustbin?"
"*Much* bigger."
"Well, they're getting one for Number 10."

Charlie had always liked seeing what people threw out in their dustbins. So he's thrilled to find the toy of his dreams among the rubbish in the skip. But during the night, someone else takes it.

The ELM STREET Lot

Philippa Pearce

"Off to mischief, I suppose?"

Mr Crackenthorpe was a surly old fellow,
but he might have been forgiven for his
suspicions. For the Elm Street gang were
always in on the action, whether they
were tracking down a lost hamster, being
galley-slaves in a brand-new bathtub, or
going on safari across the roof-tops!

Also in Young Puffin

The Twig Thing

Jan Mark

As soon as Rosie and Ella saw the house they knew that something was missing.

It has lots of windows and stairs, but where is the garden? After they move in, Rosie finds a twig thing which she puts in water on the window-sill. Gradually things begin to change.